SUN & SPOON

BY
KEVIN HENKES

PUFFIN BOOKS

PUFFIN BOOKS
Published by the Penguin Group
Penguin Putnam Inc., 375 Hudson Street, New York, New York 10014, U.S.A.
Penguin Books Ltd, 27 Wrights Lane, London W8 5TZ, England
Penguin Books Australia Ltd, Ringwood, Victoria, Australia
Penguin Books Canada Ltd, 10 Alcorn Avenue, Toronto, Ontario, Canada M4V 3B2
Penguin Books (N.Z.) Ltd, 182-190 Wairau Road, Auckland 10, New Zealand

Penguin Books Ltd, Registered Offices: Harmondsworth, Middlesex, England

First published in the United States of America by Greenwillow Books,
a division of William Morrow & Company, 1997
Published by Puffin Books,
a member of Penguin Putnam Books for Young Readers, 1998

7 9 10 8 6

LIBRARY OF CONGRESS CATALOGING-IN-PUBLICATION DATA
Henkes, Kevin.
Sun & Spoon / Kevin Henkes. p. cm.
Summary: After the death of his grandmother, ten-year-old Spoon tries to
find the perfect artifact to preserve his memories of her.
ISBN 0-14-130095-7 (pbk.)
[1. Grandmothers—Fiction. 2. Death—Fiction. 3. Grief—Fiction.] I. Title.
PZ7.H389Sue 1998 [Fic]—dc21 98-15777 CIP AC

Printed in the United States of America

FOR LAURA, WILL, AND SUSAN

CONTENTS

PART ONE

The
Search

1

SPOON GILMORE'S GRANDMOTHER had been dead for two months when he realized that he wanted something special of hers to keep. This thought came to him in the middle of a hot, sticky July night and nagged at him off and on until morning.

It was all he could think about at breakfast. He was sitting alone at the kitchen table having the same breakfast he had almost every morning—a bowl of Cap'n Crunch and a glass of grape juice. His hand wobbled and his juice glass grazed his cheek, nearly missing his mouth, he was so preoccupied.

Juice dribbled down his chin. He wiped the juice with the back of his hand, then wiped his hand on his T-shirt.

Something of Gram's. Spoon had been dreaming about her since her death. Not frightening dreams. But dreams in which she would pass through a room quickly, or be sitting in a chair in a shadowy corner, watching. At first, the dreams were constant, every night, but they were growing less frequent. Spoon was afraid of losing what little was left of her—his memories. He was afraid of forgetting her. That's why he wanted something of hers.

He didn't know exactly what he had in mind, but he knew what he *didn't* have in mind: a photograph. Spoon disliked photographs of himself and he assumed that that's the way it was with most people. It surely had been the case with Gram, who, upon seeing a photo of herself, would sniff, disgusted, and brush it aside. A photograph of Gram would not work. A photograph definitely was not what he was looking for. He needed something of Gram's that had been important to her. And he didn't want the "something" to be a girl thing like a necklace or a pin or an earring.

What could it be?

Sunlight shone through the large kitchen window, turning the tabletop white. Out the window Spoon could see his parents already at work in the garden. His father, Scott, was a fourth-grade teacher and his mother, Kay, taught art at the same school, Lincoln Elementary, to all the grades, kindergarten through fifth. Because they both had the summers free, they had become devoted gardeners over the years. Scott was most interested in vegetables and his compost bin, and Kay spent most of her time with her flowers. From dawn until dusk, day in and day out, all summer long, they could usually be found in the garden.

This particular summer was supposed to have been different, though. The entire family had planned to travel by car from their home in Madison, Wisconsin, to Eugene, Oregon, where Spoon's maternal grandmother, Evie, lived. They were going to take their time, stop along the way, see things that most people miss because of their hurried pace. But Spoon's other grandmother, the one who had lived in Madison just five blocks away, had died suddenly in May of a heart attack. Gram. Pa lived alone now in the house Spoon's father had grown up in.

"Mom and I can't leave Pa alone in Madison for the summer," Scott had told his three children early in June, glancing from one to the next to the next, then looking away and jingling the change in his pocket. Sadness showed in his eyes and in the droop of his shoulders. "Even if we'd cut the trip short . . . I can't do it. So the trip we planned is canceled. We'll try again next year. But Mom and I talked with Evie. And she'll fly any or all of you out west if you want to go. For as long as you'd like. So think about it. . . ."

Joanie, who was six, couldn't bear to leave her mother.

Charlie, who was twelve, said yes instantly.

And Spoon, who was ten and in the middle, thought and thought and thought before finally saying no.

Charlie called him a baby. And maybe he was. But this was the first time someone he loved would be gone forever. He didn't like to think about the forever part. But when he did, which was often, the only place he wanted to be was home.

Evie's husband, Henry, had died long before Spoon was born, so Spoon only knew him through stories and photographs. He felt no real connection to Henry, but his connection to Gram was strong.

With his gaze fixed steadily on his bowl of Cap'n Crunch and his arms encircling it, Spoon sat as if in a trance, racking his brain for a solution. Something of Gram's. What could it be?

He sat and sat.

The cereal had become soggy. The milk in the bowl had turned a yellowy color, inedible. I've come up with nothing, Spoon thought, and I've wasted breakfast. He frowned at the bowl and pushed it away.

"I thought you *liked* Cap'n Crunch," said Joanie, popping up from behind the counter. She had the annoying habit of surprising Spoon, turning up when he least expected it. And this summer she was worse than ever.

He ignored her, rising from the table and placing his dishes in the sink.

"You can have some of my Floopies," she told him. That's what she called Froot Loops, the only cereal she would eat. "But

8

you can't read the box. You'll fill your head with too much stuff. And then you won't have room for other stuff."

Spoon turned toward her and shot her a look that said, You're crazy.

"Do you think we'll get a postcard from Charlie today?" Joanie asked in her high-pitched voice.

"Do I care?" He did. But he would never let on. He was still by the sink with his back to her, and he could feel her presence like a persistent itch. He decided to do the few dishes there were, hoping she'd be gone by the time he finished.

Joanie stood behind Spoon, waiting, clutching the handle of her little green-and-black plaid canvas suitcase. Despite the heat, she was wearing her red hooded sweatshirt with the hood up. Her head looked pointy like an elf's. The sweatshirt had first been Charlie's, then Spoon's, and now it belonged to Joanie. She loved it the way other children love blankets or teddy bears. The cuffs were ragged, little holes had cropped up along the seams as if the stitches were rotting, and because it had been worn and laundered so many times it wasn't actually red any longer but the pale washy color of watermelon flesh.

"I can help you," Joanie offered, banging her suitcase against her knees.

"Nope. I'm almost done." His dishes were washed and rinsed and in the drying rack, but he continued to swish his hands about in the water for effect.

"Want to see what's in my suitcase?"

"I already know what's in your suitcase. Twigs."

"It's full of *bones*," Joanie said in a fierce whisper. "And I've got some new ones."

"They're twigs, not bones."

"They *are* bones. The bones of *trees*!" she shrieked. "And I collect them." She hopped with delight, a tiny hop.

Spoon spun around, drying his hands on

a dish towel. He gently tapped Joanie's head. "Just as I thought," he said. "Hollow."

As usual, Joanie just smiled at Spoon's insult, which always put him in a low mood. Charlie's insults could diminish Spoon, and he wondered why he didn't have the same power over Joanie.

"What are you going to do today?" Joanie asked.

"Whatever it is, you're not included," is what Spoon said, but he was smart enough to know that she would try to follow him no matter how hard he wished it to be otherwise. The privacy that he needed today would not be easy to come by. After tossing the dish towel on the table, Spoon set his jaw and looked at Joanie with narrow eyes, trying to send a message: *Do not tag along today*.

I've got to get moving, he thought. I've got to get something of Gram's. First, he'd ask permission from his parents to walk to

Pa's house, and then he'd be on his way. He headed for the back door.

"Where are you going?"

No response.

"Where are you going?"

No response.

Joanie slipped in front of her brother. "Where are you going?" she asked again, her voice musical, her blue eyes round. Her ability to wear him down was uncanny.

"I've got an important project to work on," Spoon replied under his breath in exasperation. Instantly he was regretful. He hated himself for being such a big mouth, so he pinched his leg as hard as he could, imagining that it was Joanie he was pinching.

"Tell me, tell me!" Joanie jumped up and down, scraping the wall with her suitcase. *"Where are you going?"*

Spoon was losing his temper. The wings of his nostrils flared and reddened. "Okay!" he shouted, giving in. "Okay! I'm going over to Pa's. But you're not coming with me. Repeat after me: I will not follow you."

"I will not," was all Joanie managed to repeat, so as not to lie. Her cheeks flushed with excitement.

But Spoon didn't even hear her. He was already out the door. He was trying another tactic. He was running as fast as he could.

IT DIDN'T MATTER that Spoon was the fastest runner in his class at school. It didn't matter that he raced through the yard and out to the garden to his parents as quickly as he possibly could, yelling as soon as he was within hearing range, "May I go over to Pa's?" His father wanted to show him the new door he had built for the compost bin, and his mother called him to come admire her delphiniums. By that time, of course, Joanie was right beside Spoon, her suitcase bumping his calf every three seconds.

Spoon gave up. There was no reason to

hurry now. He plopped down at the edge of the garden to catch his breath. He let his father explain, in detail, why the new door was better than the old one. And then he watched his mother show her delphiniums off.

"Look at the color, Spoon," Kay said, turning his chin toward the spikes of spurred flowers with her gloved hand. "Isn't it the most incredible blue you've ever seen?"

"Yeah, Mom," he answered unenthusiastically, squinting because of the sun.

He could admit that they were nice as far as flowers were concerned. And the blue was undoubtedly very blue, but no more incredible to him than the new M&M's color or the blue of his father's old Brewers cap.

Joanie, on the other hand, showed great interest. She set her suitcase down on the lawn, leaned into the shortest clump of delphiniums, and brushed her cheeks against the petals. Then she proceeded to do an odd little dance around the flower bed. "Teensy blue stars, stuck on a pole," she chirped, her nose pointed upward, her arms extended, her hands opening and closing like flowers themselves.

"You're frisky this morning," Scott said. (Frisky was not the word that came to Spoon's mind. Weird perhaps, or bizarre, seemed more appropriate.) Scott came up behind Joanie, scooped her up, kissed her, flipped her onto his shoulder, then flipped her back down to the ground. Her hood fell off as she spun through the air, and her disheveled hair looked like a feather duster.

Joanie squealed.

Scott used to do the same thing to Spoon, but Spoon was too big for that now. Although they still wrestled, which was much more dignified.

Spoon wondered how it was that he had outgrown being flipped. Did it happen all of a sudden? Overnight? One day did everyone just know that flips would no longer be a routine activity for him? It struck him that there had to have been a last flip, although he could never have known that fact as he turned that final turn from his father's shoulder. As hard as he tried, he had no idea when his last flip had occured.

That train of thought led him to Gram. It felt strange to wonder what her last word had been, what her last thought had been, why she had smiled her last smile. He shredded a long blade of grass into his palm and blew the pieces, scattering them. A few pieces stuck to his sweaty fingers.

It was going to be another hot, humid day. There had been so many days like this— one after the next—that it was difficult to remember how long the heat wave had been going on. A thin layer of moisture was already covering Spoon's arms and legs. Scott and Kay were dripping, their T-shirts sleek against their bodies. But Joanie seemed immune to the heat; she had pulled her hood on again and appeared perfectly comfortable prancing back and forth along the thick row of yellow marigolds. Her energy was endless, as if she were running on eternally charged batteries.

Scott and Kay's short break turned into a longer one. Scott leaned against the toolshed, and Kay closed her eyes and rolled her neck. "I'm so thirsty," she said.

They had tugged their work gloves off, and Spoon could see their tattoos as they passed a thermos bottle of lemonade between them. Both of his parents had a small tattoo on the weblike skin between the thumb and index finger on their right hands. Kay's was a daisy and Scott's was a ladybug. They had decided to get the tattoos the previous year to commemorate turning forty. Their birthdays were three days apart in November. "This makes me feel less bad about getting old,"

Spoon had heard his mother say to his father right after they had gotten the tattoos; she was holding her hand out before her, her fingers splayed as if she were modeling a ring. Of course, Spoon, Charlie, and Joanie had each wanted a tattoo then as well. "You have to wait until you're forty like we did," Scott said jokingly, moving the ladybug toward them, then pretending that it was biting their necks. For a while, the three of them drew and redrew tattoos on *their* hands—a human skull (Charlie), a baseball and the letter *S* (Spoon), and two red Froot Loops (Joanie)—but the phase had passed.

After wiping his face and sliding his glasses back up his nose, Scott crouched behind Spoon and placed his hands on Spoon's shoulders, the ladybug brighter and bigger than a real one. "How about helping me weed?" Scott asked.

Spoon hated to disappoint his father, but

he really wanted to go to his grandfather's house. He needed to.

"Earth to Spoon," Scott said.

Before Spoon had come up with a suitable answer, Joanie had climbed onto Spoon's lap. "What about your project?" she asked through tightly cupped fingers.

"Shhh," Spoon hissed, shoving her away.

"Help me weed later. Or tomorrow," Scott said. "If you've got something better going on, that's fine."

"We do," said Joanie.

"A brother and sister project?" Kay asked. "That's a nice change."

Spoon shrugged.

Joanie smiled broadly. "Yes!" she shouted.

Spoon couldn't believe this was happening, but he tried to see it all in a positive light. If he took Joanie with him, he would get out of weeding, a job he hated. He'd simply try to ditch her somehow at Pa's. He sighed. "May I—*we*—go to Pa's?" he asked quietly.

His parents nodded.

Spoon hoisted himself up off the ground. "Okay," he said halfheartedly. "Let's go."

"Wait a sec," said Kay. "Let me get a bag of lettuce, beans, and peas together for Pa."

When the bag was ready, Spoon grabbed it carefully and cradled it in the crook of one arm so that he wouldn't crush the lettuce. The beans and peas were at the bottom of the bag; the top was overflowing with delicate lettuce leaves—green and ruffled, some edged in dark purple.

Scott and Kay waved them on. "Tell Pa I'll phone him later," Kay called.

Joanie tried to slip her hand into Spoon's free one, but he shook it off.

It may not have been under the circumstances he had intended, but he was finally on his way. Or, to be more precise, *they* were on their way.

"This could be the best day of our lives," Joanie said brightly, skipping to keep up with her brother.

Spoon had his doubts.

3

PA'S HOUSE WAS ONLY FIVE BLOCKS AWAY, but Spoon decided to walk the long way, meandering through Hillington Green and lagging along the railroad tracks before winding back on course. He needed time to think. When Joanie asked why they weren't going straight to Pa's, Spoon simply said it was part of the project. The explanation was good enough for Joanie. She seized the opportunity to collect more sticks and put them in her suitcase.

The light seemed odd to Spoon; everything was blanched by the sun. The leaves on the trees looked dull and tinged with gray like old coins. Even Joanie's features seemed bleached out. My sister's an alien, Spoon thought.

After turning the corner onto Willow Street, Joanie held the bag of vegetables and watched Spoon jump over a fire hydrant straddle-legged. Then they walked slowly past the Frosts' house. The house was painted a rich, glossy yellow color, but in this particular light it looked dingy. Don and Douglas Frost were Spoon's best friends. They were identical twins, although it wasn't difficult to tell them apart, even if you didn't know them well. Douglas was thinner and shorter than Don, and shy. Don had a penchant for terrible puns, was forever doing armpit farts, and never wore short pants, even in sweltering heat, unless he was playing basketball or swimming.

"Bet you miss your friends," Joanie said.

Spoon glanced at the house and nodded.

The Frosts' house was quiet; the lawn was shaggy. Don and Douglas had been away at a week-long basketball camp, and now they were up north at their family's cabin for two weeks. Another two of Spoon's classmates—Alex Norman and Nate Dempster—had gone to the basketball camp as well. When they all had signed up for camp the previous winter, Spoon had wanted to go badly, but because of the planned cross-country trip to Evie's he had had to decline. By the time Gram died and the trip to Evie's was canceled, the basketball camp was filled. With prompting from Don and Douglas, Spoon reluctantly agreed to having his name put on the waiting list, but he only made it to number four. He wondered if it had all worked out for the best. What if he had gotten to attend camp and then missed Gram so much, suddenly found himself so sad because of her, that he needed to go home? The thought embarrassed him.

Don and Douglas had asked if Spoon could join them at the cabin following camp, but Spoon had gone last year and Mrs. Frost said that she couldn't handle more than one guest at a time and it was Angela's turn to pick a friend to vacation with them. Angela was Don and Douglas's eight-year-old sister. Don, Douglas, and Spoon called her Devila. Spoon was relieved that he hadn't had to decline an official invitation from Mr. and Mrs. Frost—relieved, for once, that Devila was treated fairly.

"Good-bye, Frosts' house," Joanie said, waving. She blew a kiss.

As much as he wanted to lose Joanie, Spoon knew that he couldn't. Not out here anyway. He'd try to ditch her at Pa's. At least then she'd be safe. His parents and teachers were forever sounding warnings about strangers. "You can't be too careful." "Don't think it can't happen to you." "Trust your instincts." A few times, he ran ahead and hid behind a tree or a garage, then suddenly sprang out at her, growling, just to give her a little scare.

It worked. Joanie screamed and dropped her suitcase every time. But then she was right at his heels again like his shadow, no grudges held.

As they crossed Commonwealth Avenue, the busiest street in the neighborhood, Spoon took Joanie's hand in his.

Joanie squeezed Spoon's palm. "Why did we call Gram Gram, but we call Evie Evie?"

Spoon flicked Joanie's hand away as soon as they were safely on the sidewalk. He shrugged. "I don't know," he said. He had never really given it much thought before. Gram's name was Martha, but she had always been Gram. And Evie was their grandmother, too, but they had always, always called her Evie, never Grandma or Grammy or Gram. "I don't know," he said again.

Names were funny things. His certainly was. His name was Frederick, but everyone called him Spoon. He hated it when he had to tell someone the story of his name. "*Spoon?*" people would say upon hearing his name for the first time. They always had the same pinched look on their faces. Many people had tried to guess the origin of his name, but none had ever guessed correctly. He doubted if anyone ever would.

One morning, when Spoon's mother was pregnant with him, she decided to plant some peonies in the side yard. The peonies had been divided from a plant of Gram's and were at least a half a century old. Kay had only been digging for minutes when her shovel hit something that clinked. She bent down, reached into the shallow hole, and found a tarnished baby spoon peeking out of the dirt. A young, lanky boy with thick curls, wearing a sailor suit and holding a hobbyhorse, was embossed on the handle of the spoon, and the name Frederick was engraved into the back of the handle in an elegant script. As Kay cleaned the spoon with the hem of her gardening smock, she felt the baby kick for the first time. She made up her mind then and there that if her baby was a boy, he would be named Frederick.

Following Frederick's birth, friends and neighbors asked where his name had come from. Was he named for an uncle? A great-grandfather? After telling the story time and again, Scott and Kay started calling Frederick "Spoon Baby" and then simply "Spoon." Charlie took to it quickly. Spoon, or "Poon" as he pronounced it, rolled off his two-year-old tongue with much greater ease than did Frederick. He loved the *ooooo* sound. Soon Spoon was the only name anyone called the baby, and now when Spoon heard the name Frederick it barely registered with him, barely caused his head to turn. Sometimes, when he was asked, he lied and said that Spoon was a nickname for Spooner, his given name, an old family name on his mother's side.

The spoon lay on Kay's dresser amid a dusty jumble—hairpins, rubber bands, foreign coins, beads, stone fruit. "I'll give it to you," she told him once, "when you're old enough for it to mean something to you."

"There he is!" Joanie said all of a sudden. "There's Pa!"

Down the block, beyond a parked car and through some bushes, Spoon could see his grandfather. He was carrying a garbage can to the curb.

Joanie ran ahead.

When Spoon reached the front walk, Joanie was already in Pa's arms. "We're here to work on the project!" she announced.

Spoon blushed. He unrolled and rolled

the top of the bag of vegetables; the lettuce leaves were squashed and wilted.

Pa put Joanie down. "That's funny," he said. "As it turns out I *do* have a project. And I can use all the help I can get. I'm cleaning out the garage."

"So *that's* the project," Joanie said gleefully, winking at Spoon.

Spoon sighed with relief. What a coincidence! He could barely believe his good fortune. Now Joanie would be completely occupied and he could do what he needed to do. Maybe he'd even find something of Gram's in the garage. He and Pa greeted each other with a hug. Spoon handed over the bag of vegetables, and then they walked up the driveway to the garage side by side.

WITHIN MINUTES, JOANIE WAS BUSY sweep-
ing the garage floor. Periodically she used
the broom handle as a pretend microphone
and sang her delphinium song. Streams of
light from the windows cut the stale air, and
when Joanie stepped through the shafts,
they resembled spotlights. She turned circles
like a cat chasing its tail. Dust rose around
her.

"You lighten my heart," Pa said to Joanie.
"If you had a charm alarm, it would be
going off every ten seconds and the whole
town would hear it."

"What about her jerk alert?" Spoon said under his breath. "It never stops ringing."

It was annoying to Spoon that Joanie had such an effect on Pa. Several times, Spoon caught Pa glancing at Joanie with adoring eyes, then chuckling, as if he were unable to do anything but marvel at her and delight in her. During the short span of a couple of hours, Pa referred to her with more than one term of endearment: My Sweet Ragamuffin, Pa's Little Geyser (because of her unkempt hair), Joan of My Heart.

Spoon was no competition. He didn't sing; he didn't dance; he didn't drag a suitcase full of sticks around with him, calling attention to himself. Spoon could wiggle his ears, but that was about it. Subtle in comparison. Pa could wiggle his ears, too, and they used to do it together regularly, hamming it up like a vaudeville act. They had only done it once since Gram had died, and then only half-heartedly.

As Pa swiped at a tangle of cobweb curtains with a rag, Spoon looked right at him and wiggled his ears with fierce determination. Pa didn't respond. He seemed to squint at a spot on the rafters, his heavy silver eyebrows drawing together, then he continued to work on the cobwebs.

The morning wore on, and Spoon carried out many tasks. He lugged old broken windows to the curb and stacked them. He peeled moldy, rippled Con-Tact paper off some shelves, shelves that Pa would reline later. He bundled damp magazines with string, then piled them into neat towers.

While he worked, he thought of all the ways in which Pa had changed since Gram's death. Pa seemed more bony, and pale. His eyes were still icy blue, but they were often pink rimmed and watery. And most distressing to Spoon was how easily Pa could be distracted now, how sometimes he seemed to be focused on something far, far away, or focused on nothing at all.

And there were other things. Things Pa didn't do any longer. He didn't wiggle his ears. Or tell as many silly jokes as he used to. Or religiously follow the Brewers. And he didn't play cards.

Gram, Pa, and Spoon used to play triple solitaire any chance they could get. They played at Gram and Pa's round dining-room table. A few times a week, Spoon stopped by their house for a hand or two on his way home from school; they played any time of day during the summer. They each had their own deck of cards, rubber banded and stored in the bottom middle drawer of Gram's breakfront.

"We could still play cards?" Spoon had said to Pa sometime in June and again at the beginning of July. The last time, the time in July, Spoon had added, "You and me? You know, *double* solitaire."

Pa tapped his chin and stroked his neck. His eyes fastened onto something in the breakfront. "I saw two squirrels this morning in the lilac bushes, doing acrobatics like I've never seen." His voice trailed off. "Very funny . . ."

Spoon had been particularly stung by Pa's response, but he knew that it didn't have anything to do with him. And Pa made a point of ruffling Spoon's hair about a dozen times that afternoon, as if in apology.

Spoon's parents called Pa at least once a day, or visited with vegetables from the garden or a sack of groceries from the store. They invited him for dinner frequently, and he came over to their house every Sunday for brunch. Gram and Pa used to host the weekly brunch, but Pa had asked to change it. Scott and Kay agreed to the change instantly; they were both simply relieved and happy that Pa wanted to continue the tradition in some way. "I just don't want him to dwindle," Kay had a new habit of saying.

Despite all the changes, Pa still kept a supply of root beer especially for Spoon in the basement refrigerator, and the jar of Coffee Nips on the kitchen counter never emptied. They were small things, but they were reassuring.

The garage was becoming noticeably tidy. Although Spoon was concentrating on the cleanup, his search for something of Gram's was always on his mind. He poked here and there, sneaking peeks in drawers and boxes. Twice he announced that he was going to the house to use the bathroom (he didn't really have to go), so that he could snoop a bit alone. "I'll be right back," he said both times.

On his second trip, as he was pawing through the junk drawer in the pantry, Joanie startled him, her pointy hood jutting out from behind the door. "What are you doing?" she asked.

"I told you I came in the house to pee," Spoon said angrily, cramming a nest of odds and ends back into the drawer and jamming it closed. "If you want all the details, just let me know."

"You didn't pee in *here*, did you?" she asked, horrified.

"Maybe I did," he snapped. He flew by her and stormed back to the garage.

Later, just as Spoon was about to give up hope for the morning, he spotted something promising hanging from a nail in a dark corner behind some crates. The something was rusty and appeared to be a key—an oddly shaped one. Spoon plucked it down from the wall. He sniffed it and turned it in his fingers. Orange-brown dust rubbed off on his skin. "What is this?" Spoon asked Pa, holding it out on his palm.

"Ah," Pa breathed, dropping his eyes to the key. "A skate key. You don't see those around anymore."

"Was it Gram's?" Spoon asked loudly, excited by the prospect. This could be exactly what I'm looking for, he thought. He squinted and threw his chin out, the way he sometimes did when he willed something to happen.

Pa scratched his eyebrow. His cheek twitched, as if hearing the word *Gram* had set off a small tremor inside him. "No, no," Pa replied with an effort, looking away for a second. "This was your father's. He used to wear it around his neck. I wonder where the skates are. Probably hidden here somewhere."

"Oh," said Spoon in a thin voice.

"Let's see," Joanie said. She snatched the key from her brother's hand. She held it up to the light. "Can I have it? Please?"

"Well," said Pa, "your brother found it." Pa turned toward Spoon.

Joanie jumped up and down.

"Take it," Spoon said. "Take it." He

realized that he'd better be careful on two accounts. One, if he found something good, he didn't want Joanie to know because she'd want it. And, two, he felt as though he needed to be delicate with Pa where it concerned Gram; he didn't want to upset him.

All of a sudden, Spoon's stomach growled.

"Spoon's clock and my watch say it's lunchtime," Pa stated, holding out his arm and studying his bare wrist quizzically, making a little joke. "This place is in good order. Why don't we wash up and get something to eat?"

Spoon felt empty in every way. He was starving. He missed Gram. He missed the old Pa—the ear-wiggling, card-playing one. And he still hadn't found what he was looking for.

INSTEAD OF DOING THE USUAL THING—having lunch at the kitchen table—Pa led them to the dining room. "Since you both fixed such creative food," he said, "I thought it would be fitting to eat out here. It's more fancy."

"We deserve to be fancy," Joanie said proudly. "We worked hard."

"Yes, we did," said Pa. "And I thank you both."

Spoon was so hungry he ate two peanut butter and banana sandwiches (sprinkled with cinnamon and sugar). He drank two bottles of root beer as well.

Joanie decided that she wanted milk mixed with honey and chocolate syrup, which Pa was nice enough to let her have. She sipped it noisily from a gravy boat. "This is called kitty soup," she declared. "And it's delicious. Meow."

"You are so weird," Spoon said, shaking his head.

Compared to his grandchildren's concoctions, Pa's lunch seemed particularly ordinary —a big salad and some crackers and cheese.

"We specially delivered that lettuce," Joanie said between slurps, pointing to Pa's salad. "Like a mailman, only better."

Pa laughed softly and nodded.

Except for Joanie's occasional insight— "Fancy trees wear gold leaves, and they like kitty soup better than rain." "Fancy cats purr when their kitty soup gets caught in their neck with a bumblebee."—the lunch was a quiet one.

Spoon noticed that there was a stack of *New Yorker* magazines on Gram's chair and a potted grapefruit plant at her place on the table. He wondered if Pa had set those things there purposely so that no one would sit where Gram always had.

When in the dining room, one couldn't help but think of Gram. More than anyplace else in the house, this was where her presence was felt most strongly. Gram had collected suns, and they hung all around, orbiting the table like colorful planets in some fantastic solar system. The four walls were covered with suns fashioned from different materials —wood, clay, plaster, metal. Stained-glass suns dangled in the windows. Gram had owned more than two hundred of them from all over the world. They were big and small, shiny and dull, delicate and sturdy, ornamental and plain. Some were gifts, and some Gram had bought when she and Pa had been traveling. Spoon, Joanie, and Charlie had made a few of them—nothing but clumsy attempts, in Spoon's opinion. Kay had sculpted some of the best ones; they were clay and she had fired them in the kiln at the school where she taught.

Spoon's favorite was one of the largest— a stern-looking sun from Mexico. He couldn't remember the reason, but he had named this particular sun Bob when he was younger. Bob's flinty face was divided by a deeply etched frown as thick and long as a dinner knife. A heavy brow shielded Bob's penetrating eyes. Years ago, Spoon had been convinced that Bob's eyes blinked when Spoon was alone in the dining room. As soon as anyone else entered the room, the eyes became fixed again. Bob had truly frightened Spoon, but in a deliciously pleasing way. Now, to think that Bob had scared him at all caused Spoon to smile.

"The suns are all girls, you know," Joanie said thoughtfully, as she scooted down from her chair. "And they're watching us."

"If they're all girls," Spoon said, gesturing toward a brightly painted sun made from a coconut shell, "how come that one has a mustache?"

Joanie picked up the empty gravy boat and started for the kitchen. "Because," she answered matter-of-factly, "she forgot to shave this morning."

Spoon shot an acid look in Joanie's direction.

Pa followed Joanie with his dirty dishes. Spoon rose to follow Pa, but one of the stained-glass suns in the window caught the light of the real sun and sent off pure white flashes directly at Spoon. He sat down again, mesmerized by the gleaming orb, feeling as if he was on the brink of a meaningful thought, on the verge of solving his problem.

His eyes darted from one sun to the next. Something of Gram's.

Thinking, thinking.

Taking one of Gram's suns was an obvious choice. But each one was too important in its own way, too substantial a thing to take without permission. And Spoon couldn't bring himself to ask Pa. He considered helping himself to one of the smallest, most homely suns, but he knew that Pa would notice: there would be a nail hole, an empty spot on the wall.

Thinking, thinking.

Pa poked his head through the doorframe. "We're going back to the garage," he said. "Joanie saw some things this morning that she wants."

"Some bones," Joanie piped in. "Big ones."

"Leave the dishes," Pa told Spoon. "I'll clean up later."

Spoon lingered. The sun that had captured his attention was amber colored. It turned gently in the window. Spoon swayed his head from side to side in rhythm with the sun.

Thinking, thinking.

Another ray of light shone through the window, bouncing off the stained-glass suns. They sparkled like gems—topaz, rubies, emeralds, diamonds. Spoon blinked; something flashed in his mind. And in that instant he knew what he would do. He was surprised that the idea hadn't come to him sooner.

6

KNEELING, SPOON OPENED the bottom middle drawer of the breakfront. The three decks
of cards were there, as always, packed snugly
into the chock-full drawer like three birds
in a nest. Spoon was sure that no one had
played with the cards—much less set eyes
on them—since Gram's death, and so he
hesitated before picking up Gram's deck. It
felt eerie to hold something Gram had used
so many times, something that she, most
likely, had touched last.

Spoon's deck and Pa's remained in the
drawer. The backs of Pa's cards were printed

in red with the symbol for the University of Wisconsin, where Pa had been a professor in the history department. Spoon's cards had Green Bay Packer helmets on them. The backs of Gram's cards were decorated with suns. Suns with faces.

Spoon closed the drawer, then sat on the floor. He unwound the rubber band from Gram's cards and shuffled them. Fifty-two suns *snap-snap-snapped* between his fingers.

For as long as Spoon could remember, Gram had used only these cards. The wear and tear was obvious. Several cards were bent, divided by white creases. Some had dog-eared corners. There was a general suppleness to the cards. And the jokers had been doctored with a felt-tip marking pen and substituted for two lost cards—the three of spades and the seven of hearts.

Again Spoon shuffled the cards. A feeling of complete certainty came over him. He knew, just knew, that the deck of cards was precisely what he had been searching for. He also knew that Pa wouldn't miss the cards, given his reaction when Spoon had asked him to play double solitaire.

Spoon flipped the cards down onto the carpet in rows, the suns facing up. One hundred and four eyes stared at him, and he stared back, intently.

Suddenly a noise from outside jostled Spoon's thoughts, and he realized that he had lost track of time. He wondered how long he had been alone in the house. Quickly he collected the cards, bound them with the rubber band, shoved them into his front pants pocket, and joined Pa and Joanie in the garage.

"Look what Pa gave me," Joanie said. She held up a piece of driftwood that was approximately a foot long. Another piece lay at her feet. "They're my biggest bones, and they don't even fit in my suitcase with all my other bones, so Pa gave me this, too."

Joanie stepped aside to reveal an old brocade knitting bag with wooden handles.

"That belonged to Great-Grandma Tuttle," Pa said. "She used to knit mittens. That bag's been out here for as long as we've lived here."

"Where's the driftwood from?" Spoon asked.

"I found it at Lake Michigan, ages ago when we were on vacation. I liked how gnarled, yet smooth it was. And the shapes fascinated me. They looked like fantastic creatures from an imaginary land."

"I also got a book of nursery rhymes," Joanie said proudly. She pulled a book called *Ring O' Roses* out of the knitting bag and hugged it to her chest. "I know it's too little for me, but I love the pictures anyway. And don't forget my skate key," she added.

"Some haul," Spoon said.

"Is there anything you want, Spoon?" Pa asked, tilting his head, surveying the garage.

Spoon curled his toes in his sneakers. "Nah," he said, lowering his eyelids. "I don't need anything."

"Well, gather your things, Little Geyser," Pa said. "You two had better get home before your parents send out a search team."

They said their good-byes.

"See you soon," Pa called one last time, waving.

"Today is Friday," Joanie yelled back. "So we'll see you Sunday for brunch. Maybe even before that."

More waving.

"This was a good day," Joanie said to Spoon as she lugged her suitcase in one hand and her knitting bag in the other down Pa's long driveway. The knitting bag dragged along the pavement. "I got lots of things."

"Yeah," Spoon said. I got lots of things, too, he thought. Fifty-two suns. "I'll carry your suitcase for you."

"You will?"

Spoon nodded.

She handed it over and readjusted her shoulders. "Thanks."

"Sure."

Now Joanie held the knitting bag with both arms. "Good baby," she said to it, stroking the brocade with her thumb.

On the way home Spoon looked down, patting the bulge in his pocket, checking to make sure that the cards were still there. Already he felt closer to Gram somehow. They were lucky cards. He was positive. The thought sent a current through him. And as Spoon stepped onto his own front porch, one leg lifted high to take two stairs at once, it felt as if the suns were smoldering, burning a hole in his pocket.

PART TWO

The
Sun

THERE WERE THREE POSTCARDS waiting
when Spoon and Joanie returned from Pa's
house. One was from Charlie, one was from
Evie, and one was from Don and Douglas.
Charlie's postcard read:

> *Dear Mom, Dad, Spoon, & Joanie,*
> *It has been sunny every day. Even on*
> *the coast.*
> *We saw the sea lion caves today. It*

sounded like a hundred dogs barking.
I got a present for everyone. Except Spoon.
(Just kidding!) (Maybe!)

  Sincerely,
  Your favorite son & brother,
   Charlie

Evie's postcard read:

  To all,
Charlie and I have been enjoying each
other's company. We started at Coos Bay
and have been heading north along the
coast. How beautiful! I realized all over
again why I love Oregon so much. Last
night's sunset was glorious——both the sky
and the water were flame red. We'll call
again soon.

  Much love,
   Evie

Don and Douglas's postcard read:

> Hey Spoon,
> Devila and her friend Julie got sunburn
> all over. They are the color of baby gerbils.
> GROSS! See you soon.
> > Don
> You should have come with us. A kid we
> know from another cabin broke his arm
> riding his bike off a ramp we made.
> > Douglas

Before Spoon had finished reading the last
message or bothered to look closely at the
pictures on the fronts of the postcards, he
realized that the word *sun* appeared on all
three cards in some form. Sunny. Sunset.
Sunburn. He took this as a sign. A sign that
taking the cards was the right thing to have
done, and that Gram, in some mysterious
way, approved. He wasn't even bothered by

Charlie's snide older brother comments. A knowing smile lit up his face.

"Why are you so smiley?" Kay asked. She was sitting at the kitchen table. She had already read the postcards and was working her way through a pile of catalogs and bills.

Spoon just continued to smile.

Kay tore open an envelope and scowled at a credit-card bill. "Really. Why are you so smiley?"

"No real reason," said Spoon.

"That's the best reason," said his mother.

Before dinner, Spoon bounced his basketball to Hillington Green. His destination was the basketball court on the west side of the park. First he practiced free throws, and then he practiced his fancy dribbling, scissoring the ball back and forth between his legs. Since April, he had been trying to teach himself how to spin his basketball on one finger like a top, but he was a long way from perfecting this skill and so he only practiced it at home, in the basement, when no one else was around.

Spoon's father could do it expertly. Scott was able to get the ball twirling so fast Spoon could barely make out the seams. Charlie bragged that he could do it, too, although Spoon had never actually seen him, and therefore was suspicious. Whenever Spoon asked Charlie to prove it, Charlie responded with a lame excuse such as, "My finger's sprained," or "I'm not in the mood right now," or "I've already done it twice today." Nothing would have pleased Spoon more than to greet Charlie on his return from Evie's by strolling in front of him with his basketball turning madly on his finger.

Bored with dribbling, Spoon started taking long jump shots. After several misses, he touched the bulge in his pocket for good luck before he released the ball. He had sunk three baskets in a row when he decided not to press his luck.

Sweat was dripping into Spoon's eyes, and he felt sleepy. His arms and legs ached—from working at Pa's, from playing basketball, from growing. He pulled off his T-shirt and wiped his face. Then he walked off the court and lay down in the grassy shade beneath a picnic table. He wrapped his wet T-shirt around his basketball and used it as a pillow. Soon he was sound asleep.

Spoon dreamed. He and Charlie were playing double solitaire on the sloping lawn at Hillington Green. They were sitting cross-legged, facing each other, the cards between them on the grass. The sun was shifting haphazardly across the sky. One minute Spoon's shadow was long and thin and pointing north, and the next minute it was merely a dark puddle under his knees. One minute the sun was before him and he had to shield his eyes, and the next minute he could feel the sun behind him, on his neck like a fiery spotlight.

Joanie emerged out of nowhere. "Who's winning?" she asked.

"I am," said Charlie.

"You are not," said Spoon. "I am."

"So what?" said Charlie. "I beat you at everything else. Cards is just luck. Everything else takes skill."

"Liar," Spoon mumbled.

Suddenly Joanie was gone, and Gram stood in her place. She was wearing her old familiar red gingham blouse, jeans, and Birkenstocks, and sipping orange soda with maraschino cherries from a tall, clear glass. "Make sure you drink enough on days like this," she said. Her voice was muffled, as if she were speaking through folds of cloth. "How's Pa?" she asked.

Spoon looked to Charlie for an answer, and when he looked back, the sky had darkened and Gram had vanished.

Spoon woke with a dry mouth. He could barely recall the dream's details, and as each moment passed, more and more of the dream slipped away. But he clearly remembered seeing Gram, and so he shut his eyes to try to bring her back. Although it had no shape or weight, with his eyes closed he sensed her presence again.

Cutting slowly across the green toward home, he thought: The cards are working.

BEFORE HE FLOATED off to sleep that night, Spoon put the cards under his pillow. And early the next morning, Saturday morning, Spoon dreamed of Gram again. The entire family was seated around Gram and Pa's dining-room table. Gram stood, serving soup from a large pot into mugs with a ladle. The level of the soup in the pot never changed. The ceiling had been lifted off the room, and the sky could be seen in its place. Except for a black egg-shaped cloud, the sky was china blue. Rain fell from the cloud far, far in the distance.

Gram's cheeks were full and round, her voice golden. "Stomachs have no teeth," she said as she handed Spoon his mug. And then she said, "Not just anyone can wiggle their ears, you know. It's something you're born with."

A thunderclap interrupted the meal. The suns on the walls shook. Another thunderclap. Another.

Spoon jerked awake to find Joanie opening and closing his door.

"It's seven o'clock, aren't you *ever* getting up?" Joanie said, slamming the door one last time. She stayed in his room, leaning against the door, holding on to the doorknob behind her back.

Yawning and stretching, Spoon tumbled out of bed. He padded over to Joanie.

"What are you going to do today?" she asked, her typical morning question.

Spoon knotted his hand into a fist and

gave his sister a noogie—a gentle one, though, not a serious one that would make her cry. "We'll think of something," he said. But he already knew what he had in mind.

Between the time when the new dream was still fresh and when Spoon was giving Joanie the noogie—just seconds—the idea for the notebook had popped into his head. Complete. As if one of his teachers had assigned it as a project with specific instructions to follow. He wondered if the notebook had been in the dream, too, and he simply couldn't remember it. Or if Gram was somehow guiding him, telling him what to do.

"Meet me in the kitchen," Spoon told Joanie. Lightly he brushed her out of his room, dressed, retrieved the deck of cards from under his pillow, put it in his pocket, and sailed downstairs.

Joanie had eaten earlier, but she had another small breakfast with Spoon. Outside,

Scott and Kay moved up and down the garden under large straw hats. They're thinning the rows and weeding, Spoon guessed. The hats bobbed like boats on a green sea.

"Well . . ." said Spoon, drawing his attention away from his parents and back to his sister. He gulped the leftover milk in his cereal bowl so that it had no taste. "We're going to make notebooks."

Joanie had licked her pinkie and stuck it into the sugar bowl. She sucked the sugar off her finger and replaced the lid. *Clink.* "Notebooks?"

"Yes, notebooks."

Joanie smiled, plain and clear, but then her expression changed. She seemed to be considering something, her forehead creased with bewilderment.

It struck Spoon that usually it was he who was perplexed by Joanie and the things she said, not the other way around.

"Why?" Joanie asked.

I may have dreamed it, Spoon nearly replied. "Just because."

"Is this a trick?"

"No." Spoon said it almost like a question. "And they'll be secret notebooks," he added, thinking as he spoke. "I won't tell you what's in mine, and you don't have to tell me what's in yours." That way, he reasoned, Joanie could feel included, she wouldn't be a pest, and he could still get something accomplished and keep it private. He was covering all his bases. "Let's get moving," Spoon said. "I'm going to say hi to Mom and Dad and then we can begin."

"Why are you being so nice to me?" Joanie asked. Wedges of sunlight patterned her face, her hands. "I didn't even have to try to make you nice to me this morning. Usually it takes awhile. And yesterday you carried my little bones home from Pa's."

Spoon shrugged. He didn't think he could put it into words. He didn't bother to try.

❀   ❀   ❀

"This one's for you, and this one's for me," Spoon said. He handed Joanie a blue folder and kept the other one, an orange one, for himself. Both folders held a dozen or so pages of lined paper, bound by silver clasps. Spoon had used both of the folders for science projects during the last school year. The blue one had read CLOUDS, and the orange one THE PROPERTIES OF LIGHT, in inch-high block lettering. Using a fat pink eraser, Spoon had done his best to get rid of the colored-pencil titles, but the eraser had left pale streaks and tore the paper a bit so that it looked as though the letters had vaporized, leaving ghostly messages.

"You can cover the marks up," Spoon instructed. "Use the crayons and markers."

Joanie nodded.

"Technically," said Spoon, "these are folders with paper, but we're going to call them notebooks."

Joanie nodded again. "*Secret* notebooks."

"Right," said Spoon.

They were lying on their stomachs on the screened back porch—the coolest place to be this time of day. The porch was at the west end of the house, soaked in shadow. Spoon's family didn't have air conditioning. His parents said it was a waste of energy and that people in general were becoming too soft. No matter how much Charlie or Spoon complained, Scott and Kay remained firm in their position.

Joanie sniffed her notebook, then rubbed her nose against it.

"What are you doing?" Spoon asked.

"I'm seeing what color my notebook would like me to use," she answered.

Crayons, markers, and pens were scattered between them. Joanie selected different colors of each and held them up, one by one, to her notebook. She tilted her head and narrowed her eyes to slits as she decided.

"I think purple is best," she finally announced.

Spoon had already chosen a black felt-tip marker and had begun to draw on the front of his notebook. He was drawing a sun. He would have liked to have copied one of the suns from the backs of Gram's cards, but taking them out of his pocket to study with Joanie around would have been risky. She would have asked questions; she would have wanted the cards. Or worse, she would have told their mother or Pa about them.

Shielding his drawing from Joanie's view with his left arm, Spoon pulled away from his sun and looked at it critically. It's okay, he thought. Capturing on paper what he saw in his mind's eye was never easy. His rendering was as close to the sun on Gram's cards as he could get.

By darkening a line here, adding a line there, Spoon completed the drawing. He decided against writing a title on the cover.

Satisfied, he opened the notebook. On the first page, using a ballpoint pen, he printed THE SUN. On the next page he started a column of numbers, skipping two lines between each one. He numbered from one to fifty-two. Fifty-two—the number of cards in a deck. It took him five pages.

The notebook would be his place to record his memories of Gram, his place to list observations or descriptions or details about her. He wondered if he could think of fifty-two things.

Starting was easy. He wrote:

1) name was Martha, but
    called Gram
2) collected suns
3) loved to play cards,
    especially triple solitaire

Spoon tried but failed to recall his two new dreams of Gram clearly enough to be able to include them. His thoughts drifted to Gram's funeral and to the cemetery. It was scary how, in May, Spoon had seen Gram one day, and then the next day she was dead. Just like that. And he would never see her again. He saw the casket, which was closed. He saw the hole in the ground at the cemetery. But he would never see Gram again. Quickly he tried to push those thoughts aside. He didn't want to put things like that in his notebook.

Out of the corner of his eye, Spoon could see Joanie coloring like mad. The pages in her notebook turned like wings flapping.

Spoon tapped out a rhythm with his pen on his notebook while he struggled for something else to write. Something that would be exactly right.

Finally he added to the list:

4) laughed hard (more like snorted) when Pa and I wiggled our ears
5) said funny things like "Stomachs have no teeth," when you ate too fast, and . . .

6) said "Yellow," for "Hello," when
she answered the phone

"Whatcha writing?" Joanie whispered, leaning forward, her eyes shiny.

"If I told you, it wouldn't be a secret notebook," Spoon said, backing away a little, protecting his notebook.

"I'll tell you about mine if you tell me about yours," Joanie offered.

"Nope."

"I'll tell you about mine anyway," Joanie said. She sat up and scooted over to Spoon.

Suddenly the soft density of the morning seemed oppressive. The quality of light on the porch and the subtle shift of the shadows told him he'd been doing this long enough for now.

Spoon snapped his notebook shut and rose from the floor. "Maybe later," he said sharply. But before he walked away, he smiled at her to make up for the tone of his voice.

9

"YOU'VE BEEN AN exceptionally fine big brother lately," Scott said to Spoon.

"I guess," Spoon mumbled, scrunching up his shoulders.

"And you've never liked to be complimented," Kay said, smiling. She broke open an orange and passed it around.

Spoon and his parents sat on a rumpled blanket, finishing a late lunch. Joanie had been invited to go out for lunch and to a movie by one of the neighbor families. Because Joanie had something special to do, Scott thought it would be nice for the three of them to have a picnic in the yard, in the shade of the Douglas fir. The tree towered above them, on the fence line, casting a shadow the size of a small pond.

Spoon liked being alone with his parents —a situation that didn't occur very often since Joanie was nearly always present, as constant and common as a doorknob.

The orange tasted so good, Spoon breathed, "Mmm." Then with a certain urgency he said, "We should have asked Pa to come over. We could have told him we were having a picnic."

"I don't think he would have joined us," said Kay. She raked her damp bangs to one side. "When I called him this morning, he sounded down. He said he was busy and wanted to be alone today."

"He'll come for brunch tomorrow, though, right?" Spoon said.

"I think so," Kay replied.

"I'm sure he will," said Scott. "I'll call

him later." He glanced at his watch and then at his work gloves, and Spoon knew that lunch was over. Scott wanted to be back in the garden.

There was something Spoon needed to ask his parents. Asking would help him with his notebook. He spit an orange seed onto the grass, swallowed, and spoke. "Will you tell me something about Gram? About Gram and me?"

"What kind of something?" Kay asked.

"Something nice or funny that maybe I don't know or can't remember."

With barely a moment's pause, Scott said, "The Sistine Chapel."

Kay laughed lightly. "Yes," she agreed.

"Huh?" said Spoon.

Scott slapped his thigh with his gloves. "I don't remember how old you were. Little, though."

"Before Joanie," Kay added.

"Gram was watching you at their house," said Scott. "And while we were gone, she taught you about the Sistine Chapel."

Spoon knew about Michelangelo and the Sistine Chapel ceiling because of his parents' many art books.

"Gram and Pa had just returned from a trip to Italy," Scott said, gathering the remnants of lunch. "First she showed you photographs of the chapel. And then, to let you see what it might be like to make art on a ceiling, she taped paper to the underside of the dining-room table and let you draw with crayons."

"When we picked you up," Kay said, "both you and Gram were crammed beneath the table. Gram was all hunched up so she would fit. But you fit fine. Your neck was bent way back and you were drawing excitedly. It looked so funny. We had no idea what you were doing until Gram explained."

Spoon decided he had a vague memory of this. "I think I drew dogs," he said nodding. "Flying in the sky. Through a storm."

"That I don't recall," said Scott, scratching his chin. "But I think you referred to it as the *Sixteen* Chapel."

A hairy bumblebee lumbered by like a tiny weighed-down, overworked airplane. It captured their attention. They turned their heads to follow the path of its flight. Slowly, comically, the bee moved up up down, left left right, then quickly shot straight to the garden. And that's where they all ended up.

At first, all Spoon could think about was the Sistine Chapel. He wished that he could replay that day in his mind, the way he could replay a video on the VCR. But soon his fingers were busy in the soil, his knees darkened by it; and his mind strayed to other things.

Before Joanie arrived home, Spoon weeded three long rows. Mostly he was lost in daydreams, but from time to time he caught snatches of his parents' conversations —often just a phrase or a word: "I miss Charlie," "could call your dad," "Evie," "know what the bones are about," "daisies," "Martha," "imagine painting the sky."

As they were washing up to go in, Spoon asked his father how to spell Sistine.

In the late afternoon, Spoon and Joanie worked on their notebooks. Spoon wrote three new entries:

> 7) taught me about the Sistine Chapel
> 8) didn't like anyone best (Charlie or Joanie, for example)
> 9) knew about the Packers, Bucks, and Brewers—good for a grandma

Spoon played a hand of solitaire with Gram's cards in bed just prior to falling asleep. And if he dreamed that night, he had forgotten completely by morning.

PART THREE

The Storm

PA WAS LATE for brunch. Even so, when he simultaneously rapped on the front door and threw it open, Spoon was startled. "I'm running behind, and I'm a bit out of sorts," said Pa. Then he took a deep breath, blew it out, smiled at all of them, and said, "There. Much better. I'm glad I'm here, and I'm starving."

Whenever Pa came for a meal, he sat at the head of the table, in Scott's spot, and everyone shifted over. And Pa served the food. That morning they had pumpkin waffles, sausage, maple syrup, blueberry muffins, yogurt, strawberries, grapes, and orange juice. The adults had coffee.

Spoon watched Pa load the plates and pass them. Pa's hands were veiny and spotted and slightly shaky. His face had settled, had relaxed since his arrival. People said that Charlie, Joanie, and Spoon looked alike— coarse sandy hair, blue eyes, round faces. And people said that the three of them looked like Scott, who, in turn, looked like Pa. Spoon didn't see the resemblance at all. It was too difficult for him to see similarities of that kind between himself and someone forty years old (his father) or seventy-three years old (his grandfather), and usually difficult, in a very different way, to admit that he and his siblings were anything alike.

Halfway through brunch, the telephone rang. It was Charlie calling from Oregon. They took turns talking to him, using the phone in the kitchen. Spoon was last. He was excited to hear his brother.

"Hi," Spoon said, almost shyly. "Hi, Charlie."

"Hey, Loony Spoon," Charlie replied. "You really blew it. This is the best vacation I've ever had."

"Really?"

"Yeah. It's been more fun this time than any of the other times we've all been out here before. By a long shot."

"Oh," was all Spoon could think of to say.

"Well, I'd better go. I'm kind of talked out. See ya." Then *click*. That was it.

Spoon hung up the phone and rejoined everyone at the table. He ate quickly, finishing first. And then he wandered outside— kicking at the fallen brown needles as he circled the Douglas fir, and lolling around the garden. He checked the rows he had weeded the previous day. Either he had done a mediocre job, or new weeds had sprouted overnight. He decided the latter was the case and was amazed at how rapidly the tiny new shoots had pushed upward into the light.

He sensed a shift in the weather. A mild breeze had whipped up, and it was growing stronger, stirring the leaves on the trees and causing the sunflower plants at the far edge of the garden to wag gently. It was still hot, but the sky was clouding over, drawing near, like a ceiling closing in.

The telephone call from Charlie was bothering him. Spoon wondered if Charlie was really having so much fun, or if he had just said that to make Spoon feel bad. He didn't exactly feel bad, but moody, changeable like the weather. Without any idea of what to do next, he proceeded toward the house.

Back inside, Spoon could hear voices rise and fall just out of reach. He checked the living room, the den. Everyone was on the front porch.

Good, Spoon thought. He wanted to try something. He crawled beneath the dining-room table and sat. He looked upward at the underside of the tabletop, trying to remember what the real Sistine Chapel ceiling looked like. He remembered pictures in art books of the creation of man—God's arm extended, his finger nearly joined with Adam's. Had God and Adam already touched, or were they about to? Spoon reached up with his finger and drew in the air. Nothing grand. Just squiggles.

Suddenly the room darkened. Spoon slid out and ran to the porch.

"There you are," said his mother.

"Hi, bud," said his father.

"Just watching the weather," said Pa. "I heard on the radio a storm is coming."

"We're going to have a storm!" said Joanie. "There'll be lots of bones after the storm. Broken ones. I'll fix them."

"Doctor Joanie, tree surgeon," said Spoon.

His parents and Pa were sitting in the

old creaky wicker chairs, and Joanie was scampering up and down the length of the railing, walking her fingers along it as if her hand were a quick little animal with five legs.

At the railing, Spoon kept watch for changes in the sky. He stepped aside each time Joanie approached him, letting her pass. The voices of his parents and Pa were background noise to the mounting wind.

For some reason, Spoon's ears perked up. Pa was talking.

"This may sound strange," Pa told Kay and Scott, "but on the nights I can't sleep, I've taken to playing solitaire with Martha's deck of cards—those old sun cards she loved. It's been a kind of solace to me."

Moving several inches closer, Spoon strained to hear.

"The other night I couldn't sleep," said Pa, "so I got out of bed, went to the dining room, and opened the drawer of the breakfront, as usual, only to discover that the cards weren't there.

"I've only played at the dining-room table, and I've only kept the cards in the breakfront. That was Friday night—I stayed up until three o'clock looking for them. I've looked everywhere. I spent yesterday looking. Because I've been so scattered lately, I keep returning to the drawer and opening it, hoping I just hadn't seen them and they'd been there all along. I must have opened that damned drawer a hundred times in the last two days. That's why I was late this morning; I was looking again."

Spoon's heart seized up, and then his heartbeat quickened. The deck of cards in his pocket felt as heavy as a rock.

"I suppose it's a silly thing anyway," Spoon heard Pa say. And then he thought his mother said, "It's not silly at all." And then he thought his father said, "I'm sure they'll turn up." And then he thought they began to talk about the weather again. But he couldn't be sure; his hearing had blurred.

A sharp crash of thunder shook the house.

Joanie shrieked with delight.

"I'll go shut the windows," Spoon said as a way of distancing himself from everyone. As he turned to go back inside the house, he noticed one cloud in particular. It was knotted and huge and it resembled an eye.

Pa's eye.

And it was watching him.

And it knew everything.

11

Spoon wondered if the rain would ever stop. It poured and poured, let up for a while, then poured again. The rain sounded like hundreds of thousands of pebbles falling onto the roof. Periodically water sluiced down the windows so hard and fast you could barely see out of them. "We're in a car wash!" Joanie shouted, running from one window to the next.

Normally Spoon would have been excited, too. He loved stormy days. But his mind was stuck on one thing—the deck of cards. He couldn't bear to keep the cards in his pocket any longer, especially with Pa right there. He stashed them in his top dresser drawer until he decided what to do.

Out on the porch, a vague panicky feeling had gripped Spoon in the pit of his stomach. As the afternoon passed and Pa's words played over and over in Spoon's head, the panicky feeling intensified. His insides tightened and clenched.

It was futile, he knew, but he wished the cards had never existed. He wished he could just get rid of them, erase them forever. Briefly he considered tucking the cards into Joanie's suitcase or the knitting bag Pa had given her. He reasoned that everyone loved Joanie so much that no one would be mad at her no matter what she did. But he couldn't go through with it. He also considered throwing the cards in the garbage. But what would that solve? He would still feel guilty, and Pa would still be searching for them.

Pa stayed and stayed because of the rain.

On any other day, this would have made Spoon happy. But given the circumstances, how could he be happy? His discomfort grew as the rain drummed on, and so he tried to avoid Pa without being too obvious.

At one point, Pa said, "We really need this rain. Don't you agree, Farmer Spoon?"

Spoon's face tensed. He firmed up his lips and replied with a mute, uncertain nod.

When they all played Chinese checkers, Spoon played one game, then watched from the sofa. When Kay made chocolate milk shakes and everyone else sat around the kitchen table to drink them, Spoon hung back, leaning into the sink, using a straw to sip the shake without tasting it. When Scott pulled down a puzzle from the closet and spilled it onto a card table in the den, Spoon slumped against the window frame and pretended to be disinterested. "I've done that puzzle a million times," he explained, although he wanted to help with it badly. Out the window, the rain came in long sheets that receded down the street, vanishing like the sails of a ghost ship. It occurred to Spoon that everyone might be better off if he would vanish, too.

The rain finally ended. It was late afternoon. Weak rays of sunlight peeked out from between thinning clouds. The air was cool and moist. Branches, big and small, from the neighbors' shedding, ancient maple tree were strewn across the yard. Puddles were everywhere.

While Scott, Kay, and Pa wove through the garden tying drooping plants to stakes with strips torn from old sheets, and Joanie raced about the yard collecting sticks, Spoon kicked off his shoes and walked from puddle to puddle, trying to work out a plan.

"Aren't you overdoing it?" Spoon said sarcastically to Joanie as he watched her amass a pile of sticks.

She looked at him blankly.

"Where are you going to put them? Your suitcase and bag are already full."

Joanie thought for a moment, picking at a loose thread on her sweatshirt. Her eyes flashed. "I'll make room for the new ones," she chirped. "I'm going to sort through *all* my bones and take out the old, sick ones. Then I'll bury them, like Gram."

"Shut up!" Spoon said, finding the weight of his emotions suddenly unendurable. "Your stupid sticks aren't anything like Gram." After lashing out at Joanie, he pushed her with all his might, causing her to stumble and fall into a muddy puddle.

He regretted it instantly.

Joanie had bitten down on her lip as she landed in the puddle. She pulled herself up and touched her hand to her mouth, and when she saw the blood on her fingers, she started to cry.

"Sorry," said Spoon, holding back tears. "I'm really sorry."

Pa glanced up, then busied himself in the garden again. Scott and Kay walked toward them. His parents sighed and looked at Spoon with disappointment in their eyes. That was punishment enough. That and what Joanie said in a tiny whisper between sobs: "I knew you wouldn't be nice to me forever."

12

"I'M GOING TO walk Pa home," Scott said
to Spoon. "Come with us. It might do you
good to be away from Joanie for a while."

Spoon sucked in his cheeks, thinking.
"Uh, okay," he replied slowly. "I'll be right
there."

Instinctively Spoon ran up to his room.
He opened his top dresser drawer and took
out Gram's cards. His heart pounded. Now
it seemed too conspicuous to jam the cards
into his pocket, so he placed them in his
backpack, adding his baseball glove, two
paperback novels, and a dirty T-shirt for

bulk. He hadn't a clue as to why he was doing this. "Coming," he yelled from the stairs.

"Not planning on running away, are you?" Scott said with a wink, tapping Spoon's backpack as they filed out the door.

Blushing, Spoon raised his shoulders and dropped them. "Just something to hold on to." It embarrassed him to think that his father had complimented him only yesterday about being a kind big brother. It embarrassed him to think how easily Joanie had forgiven him for pushing her down.

In terms of punishments, Spoon's parents always tried to let whoever was involved in a particular quarrel or fight work out a suitable arrangement.

"What do you think is appropriate?" Kay had asked Spoon, after Joanie had been cleaned up and kissed.

"I could help Joanie find more sticks?" Spoon had answered. "Really good ones."

"Joanie?" said Scott.

Joanie nodded. "But he has to call them bones."

"Bones," said Spoon. "Not sticks."

"And I think you should apologize one more time," she added, peering up at Spoon.

"I'm sorry," Spoon said clearly and kindly.

"Okay?" said Scott.

"Okay," said Joanie, smiling.

During the short walk, Spoon willed Scott not to mention Joanie, and he willed Pa not to mention the cards. Few words fell between them, and Spoon was grateful for the quiet.

"Oh, my," Pa said as they neared his back door. "Look, I left the kitchen windows wide open."

"Good thing your cleanup crew is with you," said Scott. "Let's go inside and see how bad it is."

A thin liquid sheen seemed to coat everything, even small things like the knobs on the cupboards. The cushions on two of the chairs were shades darker. The windowsills were beaded. Pools of water on the countertops, the table, and the floor reminded Spoon of lakes on maps.

The three potted spider plants on the metal TV table beneath one of the windows had tipped over. Dirt was mounded on the low table and scattered across the floor.

Immediately they went to work. Spoon carried in an armload of towels from the bathroom, and Scott found the mop and a bucket in the basement.

It didn't take long to get Pa's kitchen back to normal. And except for a soggy newspaper, a waterlogged roll of paper towels, the soaked cushions, and a few bent and broken leaves on the spider plants, there was no damage done.

"Spoon," said Pa, "will you please do me a favor?" He had been wringing out towels in the sink. Now he was wringing his hands.

Spoon inclined his head.

"Will you take a quick run through the house to see if I left any other windows open?"

Spoon nodded.

"If you come back with a smile on your face, I'll know you have good news. And if not, at least I'm lucky you're both here to help me."

He started upstairs. The windows were either closed or open so slightly a quick wipe with his towel was all that was necessary to dry the wet areas.

Downstairs. The study—fine. The living room—fine. The dining room—fine. The dining room. Spoon froze; he could not leave. He realized that this was his chance to make things right. He was glad he still had his backpack on. Now he shrugged it off and took out Gram's cards. With the suns on the walls watching from every direction, Spoon replaced the cards in the breakfront.

As he carefully, noiselessly eased the drawer closed, he weighed what he was doing in his mind. He decided not to say anything to Pa. It wasn't the most brave thing to do—return the cards without an explanation—but it was all he was capable of at the moment.

Right away, Spoon felt different. In two ways. Good and bad. He felt as if a great stone had been lifted from his chest. But he also felt a new stab of longing for Gram. He felt both sensations in every muscle and bone.

Spoon entered the kitchen with a smile.

"Good news?" said Pa, his silver eyebrows arched.

"Good news," Spoon replied.

Father and son were walking back to their house.

Spoon breathed deeply. Relief.

"If your mother hasn't started supper," said Scott, "let's cook. You and me."

"Sure," said Spoon, looking down, watching so that he didn't step on any of the many worms underfoot.

"What should we make?"

"Something good." Spoon thought of all his favorite comfort foods. "Something like macaroni and cheese or hot dogs." But then the worms made him think of tiny, skinny wriggling hot dogs, cooking in a pot of smelly rainwater. "Macaroni and cheese," he said. "Definitely macaroni and cheese."

The sidewalks and streets were wet. Spoon guessed that when the moon came out and the street lamps came on, the pavement would glisten. By tomorrow it will all be dry, he thought.

Tomorrow. Maybe he'd look for something else of Gram's. Maybe he'd find some other way to remember her. Maybe tomorrow would be a better day.

PART FOUR

The Sign

Monday dawned misty and cool, but the sun burned through the white haziness, warming things up and revealing a sky that was clear blue and polished like the inside of Gram's big, old enamel bowl.

Spoon woke early with a dream on the fringe of his consciousness. All he could remember of the dream was that he was hiding beneath a table and that the table was shrinking, pressing against his shoulders, neck, and head. By the time Spoon had sprung from bed and gotten dressed, the fragment of the dream was already lost to him, forgotten like some bit of trivia, never to be thought of again.

He hurried downstairs to find that everyone else had risen early, too. His parents were making coffee; Joanie was setting the table. Spoon was still saying his good mornings when Pa came through the back door, carrying a white box and wearing a toothy smile.

"Surprise!" he said brightly. "Bakery for everyone."

It caught Spoon unawares to see Pa so early—and so cheerful.

"Look at my fat lip," Joanie said proudly, rushing at Pa.

"My, my," said Pa, sizing it up. He offered the box to Joanie.

Joanie placed the box on the table and tore open the cardboard flaps. The box contained scones, Danish pastries, and sugary cinnamon buns.

Spoon eyed one of the cinnamon buns. It was as big and round as a grapefruit.

"I'm going to walk to the cemetery," Pa was saying. "To tidy up Martha's grave after yesterday's storm. I wondered if Joanie and Spoon wanted to join me." Pa swung around to face his grandchildren. "Think about it while you eat."

Everyone sat and selected something from the box.

As he poked at his cinnamon bun, Spoon wondered about Gram's cards. Had Pa seen them? If so, what did he think? Is that why he seemed happy? Would he ever mention them again?

Just then, as if he were clairvoyant, Pa said to Scott and Kay, "Oh, by the way, I found those playing cards I had been looking for."

Spoon felt a tickle at the back of his throat.

"Good," said Scott. "Where were they?"

Pa had chosen a pale scone studded with dates. He picked at one of the dates. "Oh, it doesn't really matter," he said. "Dumb mistake on my part."

Spoon's stomach growled for a long moment. "Excuse me," he said loudly. He ate his cinnamon bun as if he hadn't been fed in days. And then he had his bowl of Cap'n Crunch and a glass of grape juice.

"So who's coming with me?" Pa inquired when breakfast was done.

"I am," said Spoon.

Joanie was afraid of the cemetery, and so she said no, timidly, and stayed home.

"Joanie should have come with us," said Spoon. "She'd love all the bones."

"Yes," said Pa.

Debris was all around. Styrofoam cups from fast-food restaurants were caught in shrubs. Sheets of newspaper were pressed to the fence. Small American flags had been ripped from their thin wooden poles and were draped haphazardly across monuments. And then there were the natural things—branches, twigs, leaves, and flower petals; they dotted the soft hills like a pattern on fabric.

"Let's see how Martha's geraniums fared," said Pa.

"There it is," said Spoon, pointing to Gram's low, unadorned gravestone.

The rectangle of sod that marked Gram's grave had not completely blended in with the surrounding grass yet. The sod sat high like a plush throw rug. Spoon knew that the empty plot next to Gram's was waiting for Pa. An eerie thought.

"Not bad," observed Pa, referring to the geraniums. "They're hardy."

There was only one broken stem. Pa snapped it off and twirled it between his fingers. Petals fell to the ground, a cloudburst of red. Then Pa sniffed his fingers.

"Geraniums," Pa told Spoon, "were Martha's—Gram's—favorite flower, because, she said, they smelled of the earth. She liked the way the smell lingered on her hands after she had been working with them in the garden. Red ones, she liked red ones best."

They plucked things and brushed things aside until Gram's grave was spotless, except for the red geranium petals.

"They look nice," said Spoon.

Pa tapped the gravestone, then rested his hand on it for a moment before letting his fingers slide off. He rose to leave. "I'd like to tell you something," Pa said.

"What?" Spoon rose, too, and fell into stride with his grandfather.

"I was going to tell your parents, but I didn't know how receptive they'd be."

Spoon blinked.

"Children tend to understand these things. And old people," said Pa. He paused. "I guess I should start at the beginning. . . ."

Pa explained to Spoon how he had played solitaire with Gram's special deck of cards on the nights he couldn't sleep. "I felt closer to her then," said Pa. "As if part of her were still here."

Spoon's throat tightened.

"One night," said Pa, "just a couple of nights ago, when I couldn't sleep, I went to the dining room to play solitaire, only to find Gram's cards missing from the breakfront. I looked everywhere, even though I was certain I had put them back in the breakfront the last time I had used them."

Pa's voice was serene, as was his manner. "Then, last night," Pa continued, "I checked the drawer again—for the hundredth time. And"—Pa looked down at Spoon and smiled—"the cards were there. They were back. Either I'm crazy," said Pa, "or it was a sign. A sign from Gram."

Pa hugged himself. "I hesitated telling anyone, but I really wanted to . . ."

"Oh," Spoon whispered.

"To let someone know . . ."

Silence.

"What do you think?" said Pa.

Spoon opened his mouth, and what came out was a thin, quivery noise that sounded like *mmm*.

"I know you loved her a lot, too," said Pa.

They were near the entrance to the cemetery, near the massive stone wall and elaborate arched gate. Whenever Spoon rode by on his bike, he thought that if there were such a thing as heaven, this is what it would look like when you arrived. The mysteriousness and solemnity of the place were palpable. And so was Spoon's sadness, although he tried to hide it.

"I know it's a lot to think about," said Pa.

It occurred to Spoon how different his life might be right now if he had slipped the cards under the couch or tucked them behind the toaster in the kitchen.

"We don't have to talk about it," said Pa. "I'm happy."

There had been times in Spoon's life when he had been unaccountably sad or fleetingly sad, but this was different. This sadness was overwhelming and specific, and unlike his sadness over Gram's death, was caused by his own actions. For Pa's sake, Spoon desperately hoped that, as in a movie, some miracle would take place and Gram's image would materialize in the clouds or in the leaves on the trees, or that every tombstone they passed on their way out of the cemetery would magically read MARTHA.

Pa began to hum, something low and lovely.

Spoon closed his eyes so tightly for a few seconds, he saw orange neon spots behind his eyelids. "I did it," he said. "It was me. I took the cards and then I put them back."

He spoke slowly, with reluctance. As best he could, Spoon told Pa everything about Gram's cards.

They were out of the cemetery, onto the city sidewalk, when Spoon finished speaking. His eyes were pink; his cheeks were flushed.

Pa set his mouth and turned from him. "Oh," he said softly, nodding. "I see."

A siren blared close by.

And then Pa said, "It's okay. Everything's okay." He tousled Spoon's hair, and laughed. The laugh was gentle and sweet and meant to ease. "At least I know I'm not crazy."

NEITHER SPOON NOR Pa said another word until they reached Pa's house. "Come in," said Pa. "There's something I'd like to give you."

"I'm sorry," Spoon repeated in a small voice while Pa fumbled with his key ring.

"No need to apologize," Pa told Spoon. And then he muttered, "Stupid keys," looking somewhat stricken. His breath came in short huffs.

Casting his gaze downward, Spoon knew that the keys weren't the problem.

Pa finally found the house key and opened the door.

The something was a photograph. It was creased. Black and white. Small. Square.

"She must be about your age in that picture," said Pa. "That's why I thought you'd like it. It's probably funny to imagine your grandmother as a young girl."

Spoon was too preoccupied to consider this. In the photograph, Gram was smiling directly at the camera, holding up both of her hands, displaying the mittens she was wearing. She was outside, bundled up in a fur coat and a fur hat. The fur framed her dark eyes and her white teeth. Snow surrounded her completely, but because there was nothing else in the photograph—not a branch, a porch railing, bushes, houses, a snowman—the snow could easily have been mistaken for a magnificent cloud, and Gram for a girl angel, a heavenly creature.

"It's something to remember her by," said

Pa. "I thought of it on the way home from the cemetery."

"Thank you, Pa." Spoon didn't have the heart to tell his grandfather that a photograph was not what he had been looking for.

"I've got something for Joanie, too," said Pa. "Another knitting bag for her stick collection." Pa left the kitchen and came right back with the bag, similar to the other one, and a yellowed piece of paper folded in half. He set them both on the table and sat down again next to Spoon. The bag was tawny brocade with wooden handles. "I found it in the hall closet while I was searching for the cards. She'll like it."

"She will," Spoon agreed.

"The photograph I gave you was tucked inside," said Pa, tipping his chin toward the bag, "along with several pattern books for mittens. I'm going to give the books to Mrs. Raymond, down the street. She knits."

Spoon nodded.

"Most interesting, though," said Pa, "was this. This was in there, too." He unfolded the piece of paper and smoothed it gently.

A hand had been traced onto the paper. The hand of a child. The tracing was labeled MARTHA'S HAND and dated in spidery, adult penmanship at the top of the page.

"According to the date," said Pa, "she was ten years old. I think Great-Grandma Tuttle made the outline of Gram's hand to gauge the size of the mittens she was knitting for her."

Pa pushed the paper along the table to Spoon. Looking at it, Spoon was reminded of how, when he was younger, he would trace around his hand on paper. Then, with crayons, he'd turn the outline into a Thanksgiving turkey, using the thumb as the turkey's head and the other four fingers as the feathers.

This tracing, Gram's tracing, had been

done in a light pencil line. A thicker, coarse capital letter *M* had been inscribed sideways across the palm. Following the *M* were the smaller lowercase letters *a-r-t-h-a*, curving up along the thumb. In the same childlike printing, at the base of the hand was written: "M is always for Martha."

Spoon ran his finger over the *M*. "Why did Gram write her name on the hand and make the *M* so big?" he wondered aloud.

Pa's eyebrows rose and dropped. "I guess she liked her name," he said, chuckling.

Spoon held his hand directly over the tracing. His shadow fell on Gram's hand.

"Yours is much bigger," Pa observed.

"And we're the same age," Spoon whispered, flexing his fingers. The shadow moved like a wing.

"I'm going to put it in one of the photo albums," said Pa. "But I wanted to show it to you. You may look at it anytime you want." Pa sighed, then yawned. "All of a sudden, I'm feeling weary. I think I need a nap."

Spoon pursed his lips and nodded. "Okay," he said meekly. He felt the urge to apologize again.

"Let me put Joanie's bag in a paper grocery sack," Pa said, sliding his chair back. "Not the most manly thing to be toting along the street."

They walked through the dining room to the front door. Pa led, and Spoon followed in a shadowy, unsure way. When he passed the breakfront, Spoon wondered about the cards. He wondered if he'd ever play with them again. He missed having them and worried that his dreams of Gram would end now.

At the door, Pa said, "I hope you like the photograph."

"I do," Spoon replied. "I do."

Holding it gingerly, Spoon studied the photograph on the way home. He held it in his right hand, away from his body, then close to it; he couldn't decide which was safer. Because he was so absorbed by the photograph, he forgot about the knitting bag under his left arm and dropped it twice.

Block after block, he became more aware of how, by looking at the writing on the hand tracing, he had gotten a glimpse into the workings of his grandmother's mind from when she was his age. The girl in the photograph. Imagine that!

"Mr. Spoon!" someone called from behind him.

Spoon jerked around. It was old Mr. Washburn, waving from a lawn chair in his yard.

"How's your grandfather?" he asked, peeling off his familiar brown cap and wiping his gleaming bald head with a handkerchief.

"Okay," Spoon called back. "Good," he added in a louder voice, moving on.

And he hoped he wasn't lying. He hoped

Pa was okay. Pa had looked so disappointed when he had found out that his sign was nothing more than an unfortunate misunderstanding. Spoon wondered if a sign was really possible. If he looked carefully enough, maybe *he'd* see something meaningful—a sign. Then he could tell Pa and make him feel better. Although he had to admit to himself, if he did see something there was no guarantee that Pa would believe him. Why should he? Spoon wouldn't blame Pa if he didn't. After all, Spoon had taken the cards and caused all the trouble to begin with.

He dropped the knitting bag again.

At home, Spoon ran up to his room without announcing his arrival. He didn't want Joanie following him. He needed a few minutes' peace.

First he slipped the photograph of Gram into the pocket of his notebook. And then he wrote a new entry:

10) was exactly my age once
    (sounds stupid, but is
    important)

Satisfied, he went downstairs. His parents and Joanie were in the yard.

"I'm home!" he yelled from the screened back porch. "And, Joanie, I've got something for you."

Joanie let go of the flowers she was holding and darted to the porch. "What is it?" she asked, her voice expectant, breaking.

"Close your eyes and hold out your hands," Spoon instructed.

Joanie's hands were dimpled and pink, and Spoon noticed what he never had before. His heart skipped a beat.

Formed by the natural creases in each of his sister's hands was the letter *M*.

Spoon turned his own hands, opening them flat, palms up. Like a miracle, he had them, too. An *M* etched into each of his hands. Just like Gram's hand tracing.

M is always for Martha.

It meant something to him, something beyond words. He curled both of his hands into tight fists. His thoughts were racing.

"What are you doing?" Joanie asked, shifting from foot to foot. "Is this a trick? I can't keep my eyes closed much longer."

"Okay, okay," said Spoon, rechecking his hands and hers to make sure he had seen what he thought he had. He had.

Quickly Spoon took the knitting bag out of the paper sack and hooked the wooden handles onto Joanie's fingers. "This is from Pa," he told her. "For your bones."

"Yippee!" Joanie shouted when she opened her eyes.

Spoon's heart tensed with secret glee. And then he had a glad lifting feeling. The feeling was so strong, it wouldn't have surprised him if he suddenly began to rise toward the ceiling, buoyant with the knowledge that his search was truly over.

15

IN THE DREAM, he was running through a large grassy field. It was raining. Far in the distance, the horizon line was curved. Gradually the rain stopped and the clouds dissipated to expose a luminous, blue-domed sky onto which portraits of everyone he loved had been painted. Joanie with her suitcase. Charlie and Evie by crashing waves. His parents knee-deep in a flowering garden. Pa beside a gravestone. And Gram, alone, and off to the side, engulfed by the blue sky and nothing else. They all looked too real to have been painted. But none spoke. None moved. And then Gram reached down. Spoon ran faster and faster toward her. He extended his hand. As their fingers touched, he woke up. The morning sun flooded his room, warmed his face. Spoon lay in bed, feeling as if he had just returned home from a good, long trip.

For two days, Spoon lived with his secret, his sign. He had examined his hands so many times that the *M*s seemed so obvious and clear now. It puzzled him that he had never noticed them before.

Directly after he had discovered the *M*s on his and Joanie's hands, Spoon had gone out to the garden to his parents. "Slap me five," he had said to his father, "Gimme some skin," he had said to his mother, not looking at their eyes, but at the network of lines on their palms as they held them out for reciprocal slaps. He had to tip his head to see them, but they were there. M is always for Martha, he thought.

He hadn't shared his secret with anyone. Having it all to himself made him feel strangely smart and confident in a way he had never known before. He guessed that Charlie felt something similar all the time just by virtue of being oldest. But this was more important.

Spoon decided that Pa should know. It was simply a matter of time before he told him. Sometimes he worried that it wouldn't mean as much to Pa as the reappearance of Gram's cards had. But this was real.

And mysterious.

And magical.

In his notebook, Spoon traced his hand and dated it, disregarding the column of numbers. Then he skipped ahead to number fifty-two:

52) M is always for Martha

✻ ✻ ✻

On Thursday, Pa stopped by. Spoon happened to be on the porch, reading, sipping water from a glass.

"Pa," said Spoon, lifting his head.

"I was hoping you'd be here," said Pa, shielding his eyes from the glare.

Spoon closed his book and shoved it aside.

Before Pa sat down, he took something from his shirt pocket. It was the deck of cards.

"It means a lot to me to know how badly you wanted these," Pa told Spoon. His knees cracked as he lowered himself onto the steps beside Spoon. He held the deck of cards in one hand and extended it toward Spoon. "Here. Yours."

Spoon's face became taut. He reached for the deck of cards. The cards covered much of Pa's hand, but the parts that showed were crisscrossed with deep lines and creases. More lines and creases than Spoon had ever

seen on a hand. He imagined the *M* beneath
the cards. He imagined telling Pa all about
his discovery.

A light breeze roused the leaves overhead
and kept them fluttering. Patches of sunshine
speckled Pa's hand, Spoon's fingers, the
cards.

"You should keep the cards," Spoon said
firmly, drawing his hand back, his face loos-
ening. "Remember, I've got my photograph."

Without hesitation, Pa closed his fingers
tightly around the cards. "I love you."

"Me, too . . . I mean . . . you know."

"I know."

Everything was quiet and still for a min-
ute. And then, at the same time, both spoke.
Pa said, "Why don't we play—"
Spoon said, "Pa, would you play—"
"Sorry," said Spoon. "Go on."
"No," said Pa. "What were you saying?"
Spoon shook his head.

"Did it have something to do with these?" Pa asked, rotating the cards in his hand.

They exchanged looks. They laughed.

"Will you?" asked Pa.

"If you will," Spoon replied.

"We'll need another deck of cards for double solitaire," Pa reminded Spoon.

"We've got lots."

"We can take turns using these," said Pa, rotating the cards again.

"Do you want to play inside or out?" Spoon asked.

"Oh, inside," Pa answered, squinting. "It's pretty darn bright out here. Almost too bright." He smiled, rose, and walked to the front door.

Spoon grabbed his book and glass of water. He knew he would tell Pa about the sign before Pa went home. After all, what good was a secret if you didn't share it with someone?

Spoon took a sip of water. It was tepid

now. Before he entered the shadowy house, he tossed the water that remained in his glass out over the porch railing onto the lawn. The water made a perfect arc. And for an instant, out of the corner of his eye, he saw a faint rainbow reaching up, up toward the sun.